Fancy Farm Fables

A Kind Deed is a Good Deed

Mary Ashley Langley & Angela M. Hayes

LifeRich Publishing is a registered trademark of The Reader's Digest Association, Inc.

LifeRich Publishing books may be ordered through booksellers or by contacting:

LifeRich Publishing
1663 Liberty Drive
Bloomington, IN 47403
www.liferichpublishing.com
844-686-9607

ISBN: 978-1-4897-3245-3 (sc)
978-1-4897-3247-7 (hc)
978-1-4897-3246-0 (e)

Print information available on the last page.

LifeRich Publishing rev. date: 12/10/2020

Fancy Farm Fables

A Kind Deed is a Good Deed

As we once again travel far past the Forever Forest and over the Rolling Hills one bright, sunny morning on Fancy Farm, Octavius the owl was teaching the others in the farm about simple acts of kindness. He was reading the story about the "Good Samaritan" from the Bible(Luke 10:25-37 CSB).

He explained that the farm is getting a new addition from a far away farm. "Her name is Delilah the Duck", he said. "Sadly, the animals at her other home had not treated her with kindness." Octavius said sternly. So it would be extra important that the Fancy Farm family make her feel welcomed. He then smiled because he was certain that they would.

Everyone always attends Octavius' classes because there is something important to learn. There sitting on a hay bale was Peppermint the Pig. Horace the Horse, Cash the Cow, Lulu the Llama, and Chelsea and the Cluckers were all there too.

They loved to learn about the Lord and His goodness! He had also expressed how important kindness was to God, and how we should always be kind to others because that's a direct reflection of His love and goodness. When we show others kindness, we're also showing God's great love to everyone. How awesome is that!

KINDNESS = GOD'S

He ended reading aloud the Bible verse that says, "But the fruit of the spirit is love, peace, patience, kindness, goodness, faith, gentleness, self-control. Against such things there is no law."(Galatians 5:22-23 CSB).

After class they were all excited and could hardly wait to meet their new friend Delilah. Everyone wanted to help make her first week extra special by treating her with as much kindness as the Good Samaritan did towards the man who had been hurt in the story that Octavius shared earlier in class. "Let brotherly love continue. Don't neglect to show hospitality, for by doing this some have welcomed angels as guests without knowing it." (Hebrews 13:1-2 CSB).

The animals were each assigned to do one simple act of kindness on their own that week for their new classmate Delilah. It didn't matter what it was, as long as it was genuine and came from their hearts. They were in deep thought about what they were going to do, because they knew how special it would be not only for Delilah the duck, but most importantly to God.

When Delilah the Duck comes to school the next day, Peppermint the Pig has handpicked a beautiful bouquet of red-and-white striped flowers that Delilah finds sitting on her desk. Attached to them is a handwritten note that read, "Welcome to our class, Delilah! We're so happy to have you. I hope we can be the best of friends!" Delilah expresses that the flowers make her feel cared for, because no one has ever given her a special gift. It sure is a great way to start her first day on the farm!

At lunch, Horace the Horse asked Delilah to sit with him at the stack of hay bales, where he always grazed daily. He offered to share some of his tasty and healthy hay with her too. Horace has a mighty appetite, so this was a generous gesture of sharing. Delilah shared that this was so thoughtful because back at her other farm, she had to struggle to get her own food. Delilah was quacking with happiness!

After lunch, Chelsea and the Cluckers asked her to play a game of corn pecking. Delilah joined in and they allowed her to win. In the past they had been bullies, but God helped change their ways as He can do all of us! Now, they're the nicest group of chickens around! What an awesome God we serve! She had never won anything before, so she was especially excited! Delilah expressed that this made her feel included, because this was the first time anyone had asked her to be a part of something. Her heart was bursting with joy! The happy duck even took a moment to silently thank God for bringing her so many kind animals to share her new life with, for she knew this blessing was from Him.

At the end of the day, everyone was tired so it was time to roost. Lulu the Llama gave Delilah one of her special riding blankets as a sleeping mat and brought it beside hers. The thankful duck told Lulu that the blanket made her feel safe, as she had never had one to snuggle with before. It was a big relief to know that everyone had her back, because it was not like that at her other farm. Delilah realized that there was still some good left in this world, and made a promise to God that she would always treat everyone with kindness.

Early the next morning, Cash the Cow asked if Delilah wanted to please join her for breakfast out by the pond. It was such a peaceful day to be by the water. Delilah shared that it was so nice to have a friend join her on the pond, because she was often left alone at her other farm. She was excited to know that there was a pond on the farm where she could swim and have fun catching fish, insects, & frogs. The duck was amazed by everyone's kindness!

All week long, the others wanted to spend time with Delilah doing fun farm things that she'd never experienced before. This made her feel like a super duck! They laughed and sang. They played and talked. They took turns showing her very corner of the farm such as the pasture, barn, silo, and of course her new pond. She definitely had gotten her waddle back with the help of all her new friends!

After a great week of showing Delilah how God's love can shine through simple acts of kindness, Octavious proudly called everyone to the barn. There he explained that true kindness comes from the Holy Spirit, and reminded them that Galatians 5:22 reflected in their actions this week. Their hearts were bursting with joy!

Octavious continued by saying, "It's God giving us supernaturally generous hearts towards other people, even if they don't deserve it or love us in return." He ended by praying and thanking God for His kindness towards them, which allowed them in turn to show kindness towards others. On this happy note, they decided to begin their weekend in honor of their new friend and family member Delilah. They played a game of "Duck, Duck, Goose" laughing, running, and playing all over the farm! They were overjoyed, & knew that God must have been too!

The End

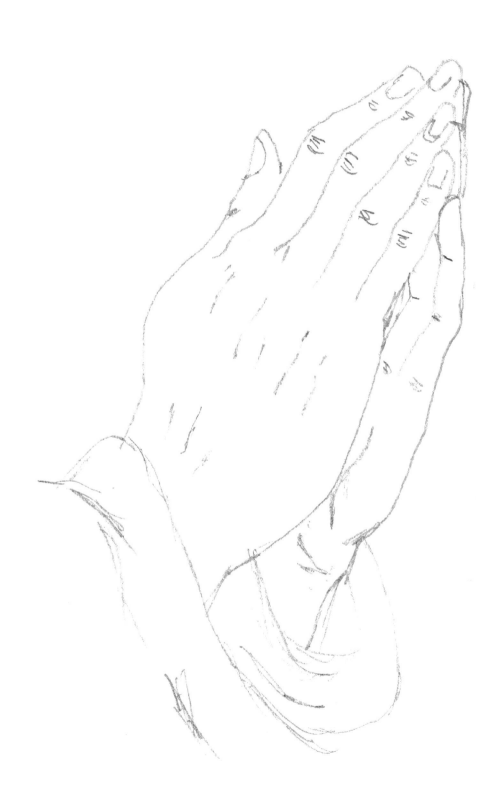

Dear Lord,

Please help us to be kind to others by doing simple acts of kindness. It doesn't cost anything, and everyone can do it. All that matters is that it comes from our hearts. We want others to see You through the kind deeds we do because it shows how loving You are. We can all help make this world a better place by being a little kinder. In 1 John 3:18 You say to us, "Dear children, let us not love with words or speech but with actions and truth." Thank You Lord for being the kindest Father to us daily, even when we don't deserve it. We love You!

In Jesus' name we pray,
Amen

Lessons on Fancy Farm today:

Anyone can do simple acts of kindness

Help new students feel welcomed at school

Always include others

Lend a helping hand

Make new friends

Jesus loves kindness

Do your small part in making this world a better place

Lightning Source UK Ltd.
Milton Keynes UK
UKHW051021291220
375650UK00005B/109